NW9529   £4.99
SER-ENG/99.

Scaredy Cat

0

WITHDRAWN

For Judith Garratt

A Red Fox Book

Published by Random House Children's Books
20 Vauxhall Bridge Road, London SW1V 2SA

A division of Random House UK Ltd
London Melbourne Sydney Auckland
Johannesburg and agencies throughout the world

3 5 7 9 10 8 6 4 2

First published in Great Britain by The Bodley Head Children's Books 1996

Red Fox edition 1998

Printed in Hong Kong

RANDOM HOUSE UK Limited Reg. No. 954009

ISBN 0 09 965841 0

Scaredy Cat

Joan Rankin

RED FOX

I don't like

Giants

but…

Mama Meow says,
it's only Auntie B.

I am frightened of

Crocodiles

but…

Mama Meow says,
they are only Auntie B's shoes.

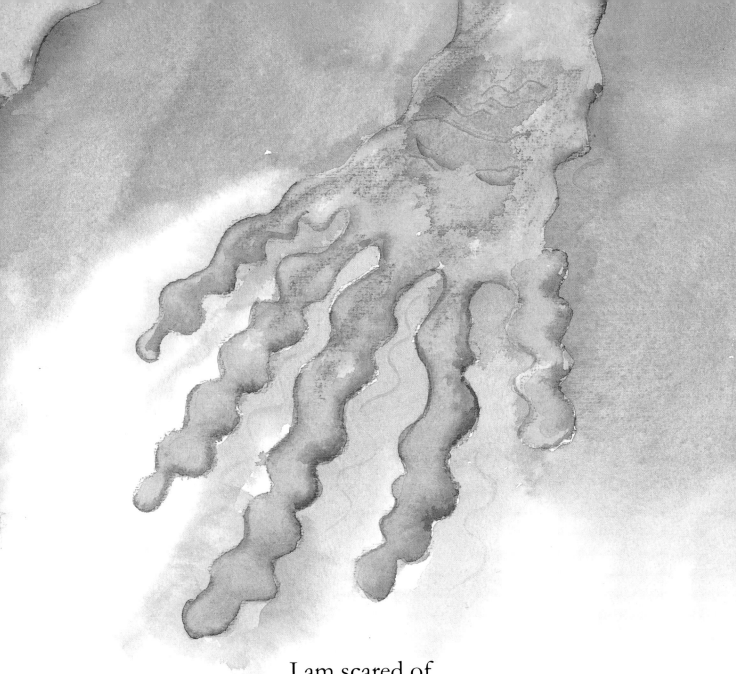

I am scared of

Wiggly
Thingamajigs

but…

Mama Meow says,
they are only Auntie B's hands
wanting to cuddle me.

I am terrified of the

Screaming Sucking Monster

but…

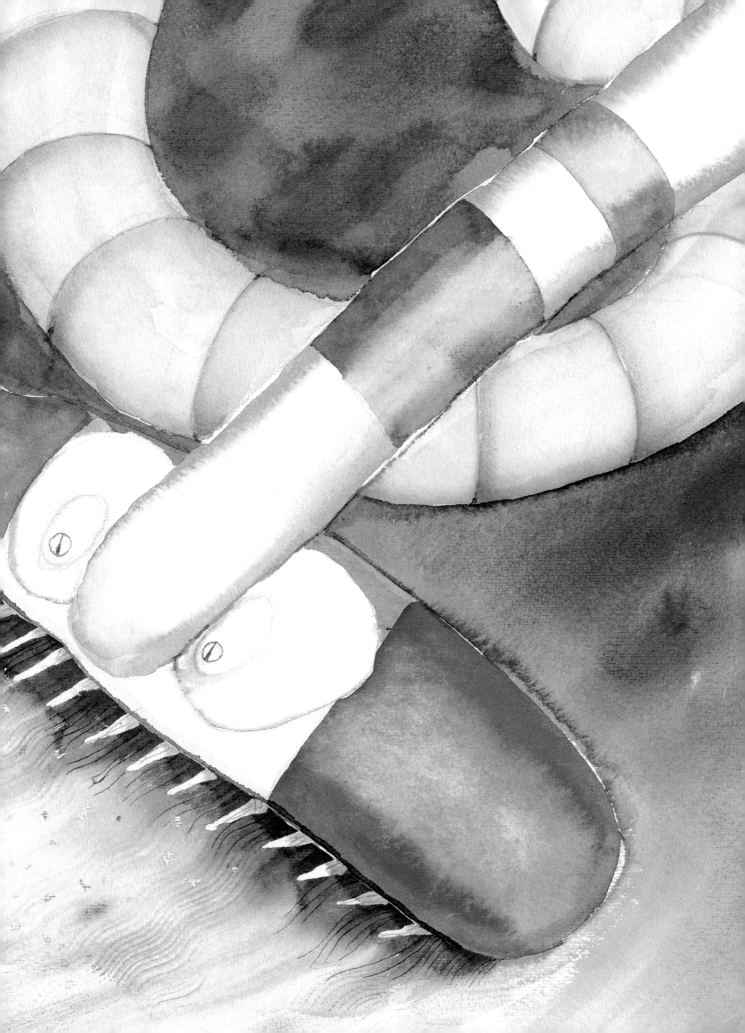

Mama Meow says,
it is only Auntie B's Hoover,
and Auntie B won't let it
swallow me.

Ooooh!

A Dark
Hairy Forest!

Quick sticks!
I dash up onto Auntie B's lap
and hide in something warm
and woolly.

Auntie B says,
there's no need to worry,
it's only Scratchpootch.
But when I look out
all I see is…

an incy-wincy spider,

looking straight at me.

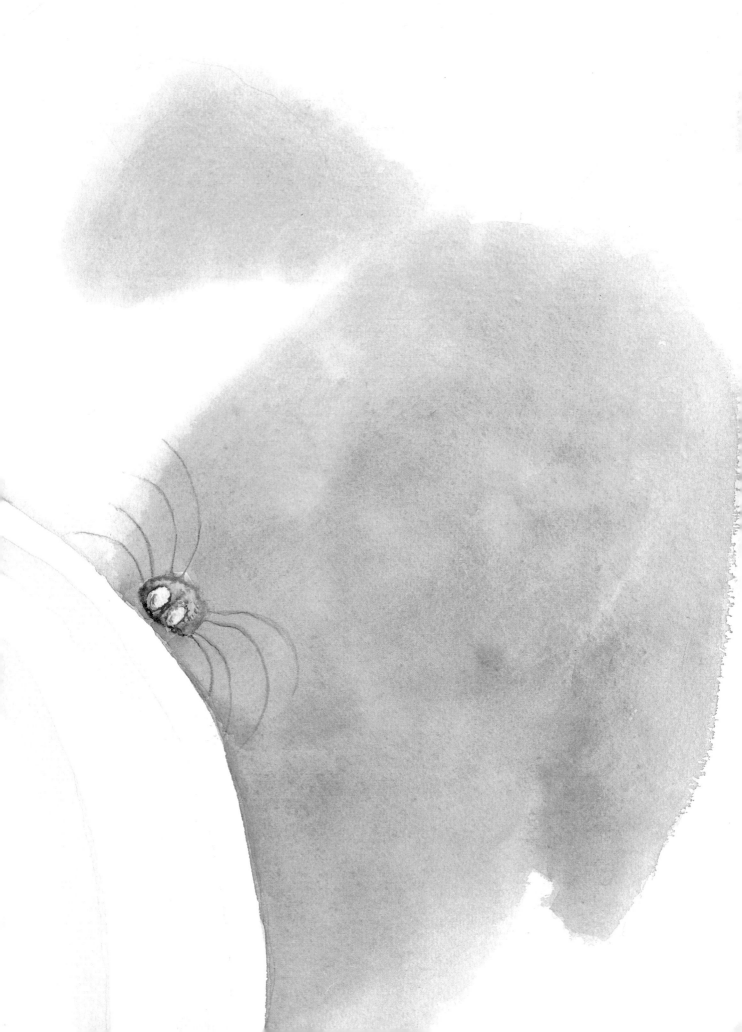

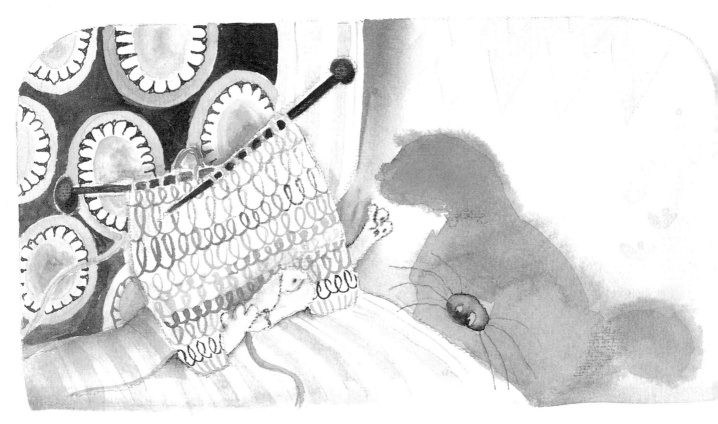

And if I stretch out my paw…

and fan out my claws…

I can

bonk

that incy-wincy spider
on his head.

Kapow!

Just listen to him yell!

Mama Meow
says I'm her Tiger Cat
because I'm not scared of

Giants,
Crocodiles,
Wiggly
Thingamajigs,
Screaming Sucking
Monsters,
or The Dark, Hairy
Forest.

And

WOW!....

are incy-wincy spiders
scared of me!